Joe R. Lansdale

This special signed
edition is limited to
1000 numbered copies.

This is copy 158.

THE UNLIKELY AFFAIR OF THE CRAWLING RAZOR

THE UNLIKELY AFFAIR OF THE CRAWLING RAZOR

JOE R. LANSDALE

SUBTERRANEAN PRESS 2024

First Edition

ISBN
978-1-64524-189-8

Subterranean Press
PO Box 190106
Burton, MI 48519

subterraneanpress.com

Manufactured in the United States of America

One of our more bizarre investigations happened shortly after we moved to our new location.

My friend and employer, Auguste Dupin, had of recent taken on some highly profitable cases, and therefore we were able to acquire a large house on a less busy street in a somewhat better neighborhood of Paris.

Dupin always reminded me that the move had been my idea, and as his assistant, and manager of finances, he was correct in that allegation. I had indeed convinced him that a nicer place, bought instead of rented, was a keener choice, not only for comfort, but for the attraction of new customers. And, the very money he paid me for my work, would be partly reinvested in our new home by way of my portion of the monthly payment.

Downstairs we had our bedrooms and the kitchen, and a section I suppose one might call a parlor. It contained three large, deep-cushioned chairs, including a ragged one that Dupin insisted be retained from our previous quarters. He treated that chair with its squeaky springs and much exposed stuffing as if it were the throne of Charlemagne and the warmth of the old boy's posterior was still contained within its time-worn seat cushion.

The upstairs lodgings, where we spent much of our time, had large windows that faced the street. When the dark curtains were pulled back, the horseshoe-shaped projection that housed the glass resembled the prow of a ship, even more so on a wet day. You could sit near the window and look out above the lower buildings across the street and feel as if we were slowly sailing toward them.

Quite pleasant.

The upstairs room was primarily a large chamber for wall-to-wall shelved books. Some of the tomes were quite old, some rarer than piano concertos composed by mice in formal dress. There was a long table with chairs placed around it, and a small burner and utensils for tea or coffee.

On the morning in question, Dupin was up early, and as usual, hadn't practiced even the smallest consideration in terms of noise and the disruption of my sleep.

I greatly admired Dupin, but his courtesy to others could have been put in a seamstress's thimble, and room would have been left over for one's thumb, unencumbered.

He banged about in the kitchen making coffee, slamming through cabinets, looking for a cup and saucer. I finally gave up on Morpheus, dressed, and joined him. The downstairs curtains were peeled back, and I could see the street was glistened by a light rain. Dupin was in his favorite chair reading the morning newspaper, as content as a duck floating on a pond, his oiled, dark hair perfectly combed.

As is often the case, he was dressed formally in starched shirt, vest, and fresh creased trousers. His black, silk-lined jacket was draped over the back of his chair. For someone who complained about our vulgar accumulation of money, he seemed to have taken to our transition far better than he attested.

"I'm afraid I've eaten the last two croissants," he said when I sat down across from him with my cup of coffee and a dry, flaky piece of bread, on which there was no butter because he had consumed the last of that as well. When he gave me this information about there being no croissants left, he didn't bother lowering the newspaper from his face.

Any other man I might have chastised, but I had learned long ago it was pointless. I also learned that living with Dupin allowed me experiences that would be unlikely with anyone else. He attracted mystery and adventure like iron flakes to a magnet. And, in his own way, he was a good friend to me.

We sat in silence, while he continued to read the newspaper, and I to nibble my tasteless bread. I was determining by what method I might manage my own private stash of breads, butter, and jams, when there was the sound of a clopping horse coming near, and then it stopped. Briefly thereafter, there was a timid knock at the door that led to the open hallway through which the public traveled. At the same time as the knock, the clopping sound of the horse started again and moved up the street.

I suppose you could say the moment I opened the door a large ray of sunshine came into the room, but that would be inadequate to describe the lovely lady that stood before me, well-dressed, if not expensively so, carrying a rough-looking bag. She was moist sunshine, for the rain had spotted her dress and dampened her hair, and a strand of that dark wonder had fallen from its bundle and draped itself across her cheek.

"Excuse me," she said, and her voice was light and airy and made me feel warm and satisfied all over. Perhaps the way a nice buttered croissant would have made me feel had one been available to me that morning.

"My name is Aline Moulin. I am here to see Monsieur Dupin on a matter of some urgency."

"Then you must come in."

I let the bright ray of sunshine into the room. She smelled toasty, somewhere between baked bread and sweet cakes.

As she entered, Dupin stood and bent slightly at the waist. I conducted her to a chair and she sat, delicately, placing her hands in her lap. My God, she was a beautiful creature, with skin as fine looking as fresh cream touched with the juice of strawberries, a mouth plump with sweet, red mystery. She could have been a slumming goddess.

No sooner was she seated than Dupin said, "I see you have walked a long way in more comfortable shoes than you are currently wearing. I also surmise that for the last part of your journey, you took a covered cabriolet due to the rain. We heard it outside. It was a long enough ride for you to dry slightly, but not completely. That causes me to suspect you live on the eastern side of Paris.

"I believe your original intention to walk, and not ride, was due to your resolve to save money on a cab. The rain, of course, changed your plans, as you didn't wish to arrive looking as if you had been fished from the Seine."

Her eyes widened. "How could you know?"

"Your shoes are not damp, and a small smudge of mud on your right thumb indicates you changed your shoes in the hallway outside our door, and placed your walking shoes in the bag. You are used to walking, which is why you carry the bag and a change of shoes. Wetness from the shoes you were wearing has dampened your bag. I should also add that you have a slight limp, though I don't believe it is common to you, as you don't show any problems with your hips or spine. It is most likely due to long-distance walking, or a minor injury to your foot."

"That is accurate, monsieur."

"To have walked such a distance, with the determination to arrive here early, rain or shine, I can also predict that you are about to ask for help due to a matter of some urgency. That part is a bit of guesswork, which is not my usual approach. Today, however, since I have had two nicely buttered croissants and some good coffee, I feel adventurous. I would add one last thing. Due to your conservation on not taking a cab all the way, and then only due to the emergency of the rain, you are hoping to convince me to take your case for limited funds."

Aline's mouth had fallen open. I watched as she slowly cranked it back into place.

"I only mention this to keep my abilities sharp. I assure you money will be of no consequence in this matter, as I am quite bored. I thought the rest of my day would be about sending my assistant here out for the purchase of some fresh croissants and perhaps more butter and a bit of jam. It would be nice to investigate something. Now, this has to do with the murder last night near Rue ——."

Aline let out her breath. "That is uncanny."

"Not at all. I was just reading about the murder in the paper, its uniqueness, its gruesomeness, and when I heard the cab clopping up a moment ago, it was easy to determine from which direction it came. That direction being the part of Paris where the murder occurred. You have been crying. There is a faint redness to your eyes. I also must note that there is a bit of dark dampness on the bottom hem of your dress. It has touched blood."

Aline let out her breath. "I didn't know. I didn't see it. I thought I was careful when I left our home. It must have been on the ground beyond the doorstep."

"I believe it is only common sense to believe your arrival has to do with the murder and that you are somehow close to it, or feel that you are. I admit that is a bit more of that guesswork I loathe tucked into my summation, but it's early morning and I could do with more coffee."

"What murder?" I said.

"Front page of the morning newspaper," Dupin said. "Beastly event. It appears a young man was heard screaming, only to be found on a doorstep with his intestines hanging out, those being pulled loose from him by a stray dog. He was barely alive, unrecognizable. His face had been partially skinned. He said to his discoverer, if the reporting is correct, his last words, which were 'It walks on heads'."

"Horrible," I said.

"I think only the stray dog would be satisfied under the circumstances," Dupin said.

"What could he have meant by walks on heads?" I said.

"Delirium, perhaps. First, let's concentrate on Mademoiselle Moulin's complete reason for being here, and let us discover her connection to last night's events."

Dupin smiled at Aline, leaned back in his ragged chair with a squeak of springs, steepled his fingers beneath his chin, and waited.

After a moment, Aline began her story.

My brother, Julien, is a man of weak nerves and prone to illness. At least this is true of the last few months. Before that he was robust and active and rarely ill.

Along with his former physical strength and strong constitution, he is also a man of great intellectual curiosity. A speaker of several languages, a reader and writer of many published articles as well as some fiction. He and I live in the old home left to us by our deceased parents. Other than our home, we don't have much in the way of inheritance, but by being careful, we do well enough. And Julien, of course, makes money from his articles and his freelance newspaper work.

His writing has led him to considerable research, and of recent he has been interested in the Catacombs, and has been to that bone yard for many visits. He hopes to write a narrative about it.

As a scholar, he was given permission to view the Catacombs privately. I have never visited, nor do I have a desire to do so. I do not share my brother's fascination with a great man-made cavern stacked full of skulls and bones, no matter how neatly they might be arranged.

Julien, however, was much intrigued, and having permission to visit at unusual hours, he made the most of it, wandering the depths of the Catacombs with nothing more than lantern light. Julien told me he liked to carry the lantern and let it at first burn bright, gradually decreasing the oil in his lamp. The idea of the lamp going out and leaving him in the darkness of the Catacombs was an odd fantasy he entertained. Of course, he could always strike a match and relight it, so his curiosity only went so far. As far as I know, he never actually ended up in complete darkness, and perhaps it was only an idea he had, not a true wish.

He examined those time-bleached skulls and bones. He made notes, drawing little maps of his location. He told me he was looking for something specific, yet he never defined to me exactly what that was.

I can only say, that in a short time after beginning his obsession with the Catacombs, he began to lose weight and develop a haggard countenance.

He was prone to strange conversations with himself, and eventually began to say that the bones were following him, walking on heads, and eating the shadows. It was not lost on me that the man who died on our doorstep mentioned the same thing, walking on heads. I have no idea what he meant.

Julien began to talk that way not long after there was the death in the Catacombs. A vagrant looking for a place to sleep. He was found in the morning in several chambers of the Catacombs, because he was no longer whole. It is some curiosity how he got inside, for there is a locked gate at night. Pardon my bluntness, gentlemen, but his head was stacked on top of a collection of bones. His limbs had been severed and placed in other locations inside the Catacombs, his blood splattered on skulls, his intestines draped about like decorations. There were odd markings made in blood on the walls. Again, forgive me for speaking so forthright. Ghastly business.

Other murders followed in the city. I'm sure you know of them. Three, to be precise. Always occurred at night, all similar, so therefore the police believe it to be the same killer.

On the day of the last murder, Julien told me he was thinking of moving out of the house for my safety. He said, I must be ever vigilant. I had no idea what he meant.

Julien told me this while he was wrapping up the injury on my foot. As you noted, I do have a wound. A small cut from walking, I presume. Nothing to it. Bothersome at best. While Julien salved and wrapped my foot, he said that when night fell, I should stay in my room and not open the door until the light of morning.

To greater ensure my safety, Julien used too much of our money to have a man install a lock fastened to the outside of my door. One that could only be opened by a key. He said there were two keys. He paid a man he knew, Jacques, a café owner, to take one of the keys and lock me in the house each afternoon near nightfall. He gave the other key to me, though it only worked on the outside lock, so was therefore of no use to me. I also had locks on my side of the door, and I was warned to throw them. But I would have to wait for the hired man, or Julien himself, to unlock the door from outside come morning.

When I questioned Julien about it, he was vague, to say the least. Said it was to protect me, and that if he tried to explain it to me, I wouldn't understand. I felt this was an insult to my intelligence, but he was so adamant and mysterious about it all, I finally decided to wait until he was ready to explain. After all, he is my brother.

Now, here is the real concern.

The murdered man you read about in the newspaper this morning. He was found on our doorstep when the man Julien hired, arriving later than usual, came to unlock my bedroom door. He warned me of the situation outside, and summoned the police. I'm glad that I didn't see that poor unfortunate. The police had him removed, though there is still bloody evidence of the slaughter on the steps. That is how I stained the bottom of my dress, I suppose, even though I tried to tip-toe over the gory reminder of last night's slaughter.

I am out and about now, but I fear the coming night. Rest assured that I will throw the locks and link the chains inside my bedroom for added protection, and after what has occurred on our very threshold, I will look forward to being locked inside by Jacques.

My greatest concern, however, is where is Julien? And that is why I have come to see you, Monsieur Dupin.

When Aline finished, Dupin made a kind of clicking sound with his tongue, something he does from time to time. It means he is digesting his thoughts.

As for me, I thought the obvious. There was a strong chance that Julien was a few bricks shy of a rue, and his involvement with the Catacombs, the constant reminders of death, had slipped him into madness. Perhaps, he had become the mad murderer.

If so, thank goodness he was aware enough to have his sister locked into her room, hire someone to handle the key, and then install locks on her side of the door. I thought it was highly possible that Julien was of two minds. One of a protective brother, and one of a fiendish killer. Dupin and I had encountered individuals of "two minds" before.

"Would it be of much concern, if I were to rent a cab for the three of us, and see your brother's bedroom?" Dupin said. "I might like to inspect yours as well. I would also like to meet the man your brother hired to lock and unlock your door."

"Certainly," she said. "As for Jacques, I do not know him well, but can certainly direct you to him."

"Perfectly satisfactory," Dupin said.

I went to my room to dress more accordingly for our outing, and when near finished, Dupin knocked on my door. Without waiting, he came in and pushed the door closed behind him. He had put on a heavy workman's coat and his dressy clothes had been replaced by more practical wear. He had on a cloth cap. He had his sword cane with him, the one with the silver knob.

"Bring your pistol, but in such a way you do not alarm Aline. Perhaps your walking stick as well. I doubt we will need your bartitsu and savate training, but let's be prepared."

"Do you believe the brother is responsible for these murders?"

"It crossed my mind, but I didn't let that bird light on a metaphorical limb. Without facts, one might allow the wrong bird to take residence in your thinking. After that, everything you see and evaluate from then on is merely designed to feather your favored bird's nest."

He went out then. I picked a small recently converted percussion pistol from among my collection of three, and fitted it inside my work coat pocket, along with some ammunition and percussion caps. I picked out my lightest but most solid nightstick, and in short time a cab was hailed, and the three of us were in rapid route to Rue —, the residence of Aline and her brother.

⟡

The steps into Aline's and Julien's house still had blood stains on them. They had been washed, but the rough stone had absorbed a lot of blood and turned it pink. Blood was also in the gravel leading up to the steps.

The front door led into a long hall, and then a stairway. Aline conducted us upstairs. Her brother's bedroom was locked. She said hers was open until sundown, when she was to go inside, and Jacques was to arrive and lock her in. She also noted that the key to her outside lock was also the key to the front door lock that led into the hall and the stairway.

Dupin asked that she show us around, suggesting we hold off on examination of her room for last. There were other rooms upstairs besides the two bedrooms, including a drafty library rich with books.

Downstairs was the kitchen, a guest room, and plenty of storage. There was a large room next to the kitchen built for entertainment. She and her brother may have fallen on hard economic times, but the house they had inherited was large and comfortable, if somewhat sad for wear. It could have used some new lumber and fresh paint, but it was solidly built, and in its early days must have been quite impressive.

We went upstairs, stopped before Julien's room. "He locks it," Aline said.

"No matter," Dupin said. "With your permission," he said, but didn't wait for a response. He handed me his cane, bent, pulled his lock-picking tools from his coat pocket, and went to work. It was effortless, and we were soon inside.

We looked about her brother's room. It was spare, except for shelves of books and a writing desk, on which were stacked some large journals.

We checked the closet, saw a pile of collapsed books, many of them open, their pages displayed like broken pigeon wings. There was a mouse hole at the back of the closet that opened into another room.

Dupin squatted, bent down and examined the books. Finished there, he returned to Julien's desk, and picked up a book full of concise handwriting. He flipped through it. As he did, Aline said, "Julien made drawings in those journals, and wrote about what he had learned of the Catacombs, or whatever subject that interested him for articles and stories. I've peeked, but it's not written in a language I can make any sense of."

Dupin studied the writings and drawings briefly, said, "The drawings are quite good. The writing is in Latin, but there are areas where he switches off into ancient Greek. There are also a few hieroglyphic curiosities."

Next, Dupin checked the long rows of books on the shelf above the desk.

"Interesting volumes," he said.

Dupin sat in the desk chair, said, "I think that we will investigate the Catacombs, and return here before night. First, we would like to know how to contact the gentleman your brother hired to lock the door for you. It may be an imposition to ask, but I would suggest you prepare yourself something of a cold supper, and place it in your room for later. I think you should make camp there, and not consider coming out until late tomorrow morning. Lock yourself in, and then the lock outside will be taken care of by either Jacques, or one of us. We, would, of course, acquire the key. As you have seen, I have the tools to bypass the key or lock you in, if the need should occur. Though I may unlock your outside lock, as might anyone with the key, I insist you do not forget to fasten the inside locks. That would make you more secure."

"Julien had the same idea," she said.

"Good," Dupin said. "May we see your room?"

Aline's room was large and had a great bed with overhanging curtains that could be dropped down and drawn closed around it for greater privacy. She, like her brother, had a desk, and one row of books next to it. I examined the titles, and found most to be of popular origin. Nothing particularly educational.

Dupin went to the bedroom window. It overlooked a back alley. He unlocked and opened the window, stuck his head out and looked down. I followed his example, sticking my head out next to his. It was a sheer drop of thirty feet to the bricks below.

There were brick walls on either side of the window. The walls rose three feet above the window on both sides and were cracked and scraped. There were pigeons resting on the edges of the roofs. They were not startled by our arrival, as I might have expected. They examined us curiously, perhaps hoping for bread crusts.

Next, Dupin studied the inside door locks. There were several. He touched the locks, locked them, unlocked them. He linked the chain, tugged at the door, then unlinked it.

"You should be quite safe here," he said. "I would like to borrow a few items from your brother's room."

In her brother's room, Dupin found a carry bag. He placed a few of the books in it, as well as all the drawings and journals. He gave these to me to carry, of course. Next, Dupin had Aline give him Jacques's address.

Aline escorted us out. The bright sunshine, the cold air, made the whole idea of murder seem unlikely and far away. But looking down at the blood stains on the steps, I was reminded of how serious things were. I wondered if the murdered man had been identified.

"Now, do what I requested of you, please," Dupin said. "We will return later to make sure the outside lock and your bedroom door are secured. But the inside locks to your bedroom are yours to secure."

Aline agreed, and after a few polite words, she found a brief, brave smile to show us, then returned to the house.

"Why did you take books?" I said, hoisting the strap of the carry bag over my shoulder. "I understand the drawings and the journals. There may be an explanation there. But the books?"

"It is their rare content that intrigues me."

He didn't elaborate. We hurried down to where we could catch a cab. The horseman rushed us to the address of Jacques, the man Julien had hired to lock and unlock Aline's door.

Jacques's address was a small café a short distance from where Aline and Julien lived. After we explained our connection to the couple, Jacques's face fell. His cafe, dark as a cavern in the dead of night, wasn't where he wished to talk, so he escorted us outside to one of the three tables, placed there for those who preferred sunlight.

There was no one outside of the pub, and there had been only two customers inside.

We bought some liquid refreshment to encourage Jacques's assistance. He reentered the café, and presently returned with the drinks. He seemed more relaxed and willing to talk by then. I think the sunlight and us spending money cheered him up. Jacques proved articulate and in possession of an excellent memory.

"I want nothing more to do with Julien or his sister. I hardly know them. I was asked to do the chore, and given a small fee to do so. I was only entreated to the job because Julien sometimes comes here to drink and have a bit of bread and cheese. I think he began to come here because he walked a lot, and liked some place to stop and rest. Said he had a war wound, a bit of shrapnel in his thigh from cannon shot at the Battle of Valmy. We are not friends, acquaintances at best, but it was a bit of money. The money is not worth it, though.

I plan to lock Aline in tonight, and slide the key under the gap at the bottom of the door. I resign."

"What soured you on the job?" I asked.

"Finding a dead man on their doorstep. Cut to ribbons, his innards hanging out, a dog munching on them? That was enough for me. I was able to beckon someone to summon the police, and after they arrived and had their words with me, I gladly left. I'm not near over it, messieurs."

"I suppose that would be a show stopper," I said.

"I suspect there is more," Dupin said.

"Finding that poor man's body, reading about the death in the Catacombs, where Julien likes to go, and the event of the night before, led me to believe that Julien was exploring avenues best left alone. That somehow, he was the one stirring all of this up."

"Explain that, please," Dupin said. "About the night before. There will be a few francs for you, if you do."

Jacques's eyes lit up like little lamps in the Land of Greed.

"Well, sir, you may not feel it is worth a few francs, but an event of last evening unsettled me such that I made up my mind to return the key.

"This was the night before I found the body, and if I had any reservations, that dying man clinched it. After they carried the body away, I unlocked Aline's door, but I was so dazed, I forgot then to return the key."

"About the night before," Dupin said. "Continue with that."

"I was due to lock Aline's door, but I was running late. Problem was, I did not have someone to take my spot here. Now and again, I have a barmaid, but on this afternoon she did not show. And contrary to my usual business pattern, the café and the outside tables were packed, and I was rushing about, not only preparing the simple food we offer, but performing as a waiter as well.

"I was making more money right then than the door-locking job was worth. I usually could manage a brief closing of the café and take the short walk to Julien's house, but on this day, I decided to wait, thinking Julien's request was merely eccentric, considering Aline's door was locked from the inside. I mean, I never understood what it was all about really. Finally, a woman I knew who works the streets, and not as a sweeper, agreed for a bit of food and wine to maintain the place while I went to do my duty.

"It was a red-letter day, I thought. Money from the café, and money from my little job, even if I was a few hours late for the latter.

"It was cloudy that late afternoon, with a patch of early moon above the city, barely visible through tumbling clouds. The air was damp with rain. I carried an unlit lamp with me, took the park trail, through the wind-blown trees, along the stone walkway, until it broke at Rue —.

"I arrived at the house as darkness fell. I proceeded to unlock the front door, as the key is the same as to her bedroom door. I went upstairs to do my duty. As I went, I heard a noise. I could not determine from where it was originating. Possibly one of the bedrooms. I assumed Julien was out, at the Catacombs, as he preferred to be there at nights and sleep during the day, but it is possible he had broken his routine and was home, moving about. I remember thinking if he discovered me at this time in the hallway, I might be chastised due to being late. I also remember thinking the noise could have come from the lady's room, or some other place in the house. I cannot say for sure, but for some unknown reason, it unnerved me. I do not exaggerate when I say the air was crawling with menace. Remember, this was before I found the dead man and was already considering giving up the job.

"I smelled something as well. The smell made the hair on the back of my neck stand up in quills. It was the strangest, most empty feeling I had ever experienced.

"I locked her room, left out of there rapidly. Having turned up the flame on my lamp and started toward the park, I sensed someone following me. I sped up, and though I wanted to look back, I hesitated, fearing what I might see. I had this inexplicable feeling that it was not someone following me, but something.

"The dark clouds were blowing thick and high, and when the clouds rolled over the face of the moon, the night was as black as the end of doom.

"I swear, I could feel something behind me as easily as I can feel the top of this table. It was coming on swiftly, bringing that nasty smell with it.

"When the clouds rolled away from the face of the moon and its light shone down on the pathway in the park, whatever it was behind me, the sound of its movement, a mushy, squishing sound, sped up. Moments later the clouds would roll again, and I could sense and hear that presence slowing. Its rapid pace seemed fastened to the moonlight; its slowing hooked to the clouds when they covered the moon.

"The clouds rolled and the moon shone. It was then that I heard it begin to run, and there was that odd squishing sound. I maintained the path by the cobbles beneath my feet, by familiarity, for the light in my lantern had faded to a memory. By this time, I too was running. I could feel and smell warm, sour-smelling breath on the back of my neck. I felt something swish. A sound like a sword being whipped through the night. I was startled and dropped my lantern.

"By then I had come to the door of my café. I had been gone long enough for the help to grow bored in my absence, and she had locked up for the night.

"Still, the welcome light of the lit lantern hanging over the door shone bright. I plunged the key into the lock and was inside as a great shadow fell over me. I had no sooner thrown the lock than there was a thud at the door, followed by a pounding, and a scraping sound. That awful smell eased under the crack below the door. I could see a strip of shadow moving there as well. Then the outside lantern went out, because the strip of light that had shone beneath the doorway was gone, and I could hear glass from its globe clinking on the stones.

"The stench went away and the banging on the door ceased. Perhaps the clouds had crawled across the face of the moon again. I could hear the clicking sound of shoe heels clicking away from earshot.

"After a few moments, I felt my neck hairs settle and my skin cease to crawl. Whoever, whatever it was, was gone. I could sense that.

Still, I did not open the door, and you can be assured that I slept little that night.

"There were two more oddities, messieurs. Both I noted the next day. My hair had been sliced where it touched the back of my neck. Sliced clean. A fraction of an inch and the cutter would have been deep in my neck. And the door to my café, you can look for yourself. There are great cuts in it. The metal skin on the lamp has the same slashes as well.

"I know how this sounds. I am not normally a man of panicky feelings. Nor one to indulge in the possibility of demons and ghosts, and horrors unchained. But whatever was after me, messieurs, I am quite certain, was not of this world."

After acquiring the key from Jacques, we assured him that we would return it to its owners. He made the statement that he intended to only go back to Julien and Aline's house once more, and that was to collect a bit of the fee still owed him. He said he would go only in the daylight, and, as he put it, "would step a careful toe about it."

We departed by cab. On the way, with the sound of the horse's hooves clopping against the street, I said, "Do you believe him?"

"I do. I think our next endeavor should be a heated dive into Julien's journals and the books I took from his collection. I think there, and in the Catacombs, our needed answers may lie. As for the protection you brought with you, prepare to bring it again later. I may make some adjustments to it, by the way. I will explain if I believe there is a true need."

We had a supper of bread and cheese and hot black coffee, then went upstairs to the library and sat in the "bow of our ship."

It was my job to examine the books that Dupin had borrowed, except for one written in Latin and ancient Greek, which Dupin added to his pile. He read Julien's journals, inspected his drawings, and occasionally pulled a book from our shelves to cross reference.

The books I was given were on subjects that I would have found preposterous only a few years back, but after our recent adventures, including one I noted and titled The Gruesome Affair of the Electric Blue Lightning, my mind was more willing to accept the strange, the unknown, the bizarre, the macabre. I knew now that a darker world than ours sailed next to our own, and from time to time it slipped from its moorings and drifted into ours. Yet, the nature of the books certainly stretched my newfound sensibilities to the limit, and at times made me enormously uncomfortable.

We read most of the day, me scribbling notes, and Dupin spending long moments reading, and long moments standing at the "bow of our ship" looking out at the intermittent wet weather.

During one of his moments, his hands clasped behind his back, he spoke. "What have you deduced from the books you've been reading?"

He turned away from the windows to face me.

"They are all examinations of parallel worlds, or dimensions. Things we in this world refer to as supernatural. Interdimensional witchcraft might be another name for it."

"Did you come across the God of the Razor, sometimes referred to as the Lord of the Razor, The Razor Lord, the King of All Things Sharp, He That Rambles, and so forth?"

"I did. I noted too that the section on the Lord of the Razor was underlined, with annotated notes in the margins. Some of the notes seem like musings, and are indecipherable, as if written by a fevered soul."

"The Lord is mentioned in the journals," Dupin said. "It was an obsession of Julien's. I think we should try and nip this bloodthirsty, soul-stealing monster at its source."

"You believe in it?"

"How can I not? All the clues are there."

"If I understand right, under certain circumstances, one can be controlled by such a creature. That he can borrow one's body, transform it into something horrible."

"Correct," Dupin said. "If, as I am thinking, Julien has somehow been possessed, perhaps we should await him at the Catacombs, for I feel certain that is where he will end up. It is the perfect dwelling for one like him. I should also note, that in short time the moonlight is not the only thing needed for the Lord of the Razor to have power. He can become accustomed to total darkness, and lunar illumination becomes less necessary, though no doubt he grows stronger then. Had that strength been acquired sooner, we would not have had Jacques to speak with."

"And if we do confront him there," I said, "considering what we may be dealing with, I must also ask myself, and you, how smart is that idea?"

"Noted," he said. "But we dare not do nothing."

After that, Dupin showed me some protective designs from *The Book of Doches*. The symbols were strange, and some of them looked vaguely dog-like, while others were hieroglyphic in nature. There were also mathematical symbols and calculations that Dupin said were related to securing and commanding The Hounds of Tindalos.

"The Hounds are the Razor Lord's natural enemies, and just about his only predators," he said. "This, of course, does not mean they always prevail. They dwell in another dimension, but from time to time, our dimensional-hopping

Lord of the Razor encounters them, or they are summoned to confront him."

"Wait. Dogs?"

"It is a loose term, my friend. They are dimensional. They live on the angles, not on the curves of space and time."

"Angles?"

"In other dimensions, what we think of as the rules of space and time run counter to our knowledge. Euclidian geometry takes a sabbatical. Things that cannot be, are. The Hounds, as they are called, are pursuers, and they and the Razor God, for whatever reason, are natural enemies."

"My goodness," I said.

"That is an understatement," Dupin said. "I will need you to trust me more than you ever have. Can you do that?"

"Emphatically."

"I thought that would be your answer, dear friend. We must now find Lim Chang."

"Do we know a Lim Chang?"

"I do. I suppose you could call his profession that of an apothecary. We will need to see him before we venture into the Catacombs, and we can only hope he has access to what these books say we need. Including Liao, a drug that comes from a rare orchid that is said to be more plentiful in the dimension of the Hounds. Some of those flowers, however, have been seeded in this dimension by cross-pollination due to travelers traversing into our universe."

"That happens a lot?"

"Hard to say, but it happens."

"I think I might need a nap, Dupin, because none of this is making sense."

"It will. Eventually."

We walked out on the street and along it until we found an empty cab. We waved it down, climbed in. Dupin told the driver the address.

The horse's hooves beat out a rhythm so consistent it was almost hypnotic. I found myself nearly drifting off to sleep.

In what seemed short time, we arrived at a Chinese butcher shop positioned on a back-street near a barber and a knick-knack shop. The street was mostly an alley with heaved bricks and stacks of old and fresh horse manure in need of shoveling and it was ripe with a nose-twitching odor. The butcher shop that Dupin led us into was less odiferous, but I smelled a bit of dried blood.

Dupin did not pause at the counter, and the young and highly attractive Chinese woman sitting behind it nodded at him with recognition. I was amazed at how many people he knew that I was unaware of.

We went through a row of hanging ducks, then through a beaded curtain over a doorway, and into the back of the shop. There were shelves full of bottles of assorted colors and cloth bags on pegs and little white boxes stacked about. The path between the shelves was so narrow we had to tilt our shoulders inward to pass through.

In the back of the shop, a slim Chinese man with short graying hair wearing a black suit sprinkled with cigarette ash, and a white shirt, was behind a counter grinding something to powder in a stone bowl with a stone pestle.

The man glanced up, grinned slightly at Dupin.

"Hello, Lim Chang," Dupin said.

"Well, if it isn't my detective friend, who only seems to visit when he needs something. Tell me you have come by to chat and not ask for a favor. Perhaps play chess, or backgammon, maybe a bit of Chinese checkers."

Lim Chang had a very Parisian manner, and in my narrow view did not fit my idea of a Chinese, who I had somehow envisioned as wearing plaited pigtails, a silk gown, and a coolie hat. This was another reason I enjoyed being a friend to Dupin. He was often introducing me to people who defied my expectations. I think a person needs that.

Lim Chang put aside the pestle and shook Dupin's hand.

Dupin said, "I am here to give you my good tidings and ask for that favor you dread, but since I'm always paying you for those so-called favors, can they truly be recognized as such?"

"Ah, you have me there. My favors do cost. And who is this gentleman with a heavy cane and a pistol under his coat?"

I thought I had the gun well-concealed, but Lim Chang obviously had an eye for such a thing, and this gave me cause to consider he might be a tougher character than he appeared at first observation.

I introduced myself. He nodded at me, reached across the counter, and shook my extended hand. It was a firm handshake.

"What exactly is this expensive favor you need, Detective?"

"I did not suggest it should be expensive," Dupin said.

"But I did."

"Very well. Name your price when I ask the favor."

Lim Chang placed both hands on the edge of the counter and waited.

"First," Dupin said, "I need a large amount of the Liao plant."

"That is rare, my friend. And hard to come by."

"I know. Do you have any?"

"It's expensive."

"I know that too. Do you have any?"

"Perhaps not as much as you would like, but yes. I have some."

Lim Chang named the price.

"Slightly dear, but very well. Also, I need Bulgarian verbena root, loosely chopped, not ground."

"Interesting," Lim Chang said. "I am sensing you have a dark deed to perform."

"I'll need wolfsbane, and dirt containing red worms dug from a fairly fresh grave."

"That I can arrange. Someone has always died the day before the dirt and worms are needed. But, of course, there will need to be travel expenses to the cemetery, and a bit more added because I'll be taking quite a chance, digging tonight, for it must be tonight."

"You're right," Dupin said. "I can get that myself."

"Never mind, I'll forgo the travel expenses."

I smiled. These two liked to play one another.

"I will also need an exorcism potion, not for a specific religion, but specific to the deed in general. And I need two pairs of those special blue lens glasses from Tibet."

"Both items easily supplied."

"I'll also need some power papers and some good strong lucifers."

"I may have to prepare the papers, and I can't have them sooner than the day after."

"Would an extra ten francs allow them to be produced faster, like say tomorrow afternoon?"

"It would."

"And what I would like, delivery fee included, is for these items to be brought to my new address, which I will give to you, tomorrow afternoon. Is it a deal?"

"It is," Lim Chang said.

They shook hands again, and Lim Chang shook my hand, and Dupin said, "And one more thing. Might I get some pork cuts thrown in for free? Enough for our dinner tonight."

"For free?"

"I think I will be overcharged enough you should do that without complaint. And besides, I know you will work their price into my order anyway."

"That's true. The cuts will be included."

"Not the old meat I smell in there. Fresh."

"I suppose that too can be arranged."

"Good," Dupin said. "Oh, and a pound of mashed garlic."

The next afternoon the attractive Chinese lady I had seen at the counter in the butcher shop arrived by cabriolet with the goods Dupin had ordered. He met her outside our apartment, and I watched them through the downstairs window.

They were remarkably friendly, and I realized once again there were many facets of Dupin's character and experience I was unaware of. Including that he seemed to have plenty of money, much more than I knew about, as well as an unexpected way with the ladies.

The lady and Dupin touched hands as the goods were passed, and after Dupin gave her the payment, she leaned forward and gave Dupin a kiss on the cheek. She returned to the waiting cabriolet, and away the horse did trot.

When Dupin came inside, I said, "So, you and that lady are quite friendly."

"Quite." And that was the end of that.

We had a supper of pork chops that Dupin prepared with some of the garlic he had asked for, but we had nothing with it in the way of side dishes, and Dupin said we should have no wine. He said we should be fed, but not stuffed, and certainly not even faintly intoxicated.

After our small supper, upstairs, Dupin laid out all the items he had purchased on the table and studied them carefully. The roots and plants had been made into powder. There were salves, and a container of dirt and the earthworms.

Dupin pointed. "I'll need you to bring me the thick, dark volume at the end of the bottom row of books."

I found the book, and was surprised to see the author was none other than August Dupin.

"You wrote a book on mathematics?"

"Euclidian theory, and suggestions on unknown angles. Even though I wrote it, I find it necessary to consult it from time to time."

"Unknown angles. Pray tell what are we doing?"

"As I have said, there are dimensions where there are angles and shapes that defy the human eye. Sometimes those shapes exist in our dimension, but they go unseen for the most part. I'm going to stop there, as I'm certain that has already bounced off your forehead and flown."

For the next couple of hours, Dupin mashed worms, sifted dirt, along with the worms, mixed the items, carefully measuring what went where. Then he sliced and chopped the garlic so that the smell of it was strong in the room. He placed these pieces in two small bags with fragments of Liao. The bags had cords fastened to them. He placed one of the cord loops around his neck, then one around mine. My eyes immediately watered.

"Might as well get used to it ahead of time," he said.

He went about preparing the other items, said, "The razor came from the Catacombs. It was hidden there. That is suggested in one of Julien's books, and there are drawings of it. That is why he was going there. Curiosity or perhaps a search for power. Thing is, you do not play with the razor. It is there as a temptation, and if you find it, and take it, or should it cut you, it owns you. Julien worked for months to find it. Truth is, there is more than one razor, existing simultaneously due to the vagaries of time and dimensional travel. All of them belong to the Lord. Sharp things in general are the tools of his kingdom. In his world he is a god. Here, he is an abomination."

"I read about him, but I never could get an understanding on exactly what he was," I said.

"He is everything wicked. He is a dark, top-hatted thing with razor nails, needle-thin, impossibly sharp, shiny teeth. His clothes are made of human flesh. His feet are hooves, and he wears decapitated heads for shoes, sticking his hooved feet into the mouths of those heads. Remember Jacques's story, hearing the squishing behind him. The shading of the moon can weaken him, but it doesn't entirely diminish him, and as I was saying, in time, it no longer matters. And the Catacombs. Being amongst the dead he gains greater strength. Oh, we'll need lanterns."

Before our departure, I prepared some tea, and brought a cup to Dupin, who was seated at the long table, his head turned toward the window, rain splattering against it. He had one of Julien's journals in his lap. He set it on the table and pushed it toward me.

"Here. There are some extracts I would like you to read from Julien's notes. I've marked them. This section deals with the Catacombs, so you are being dropped into the middle of it. Sit and read."

There were pieces of torn paper placed amongst the pages as markers. I sat, sipped my tea, and read.

JULIEN'S DIARY

...my initial skepticisms were solidified into absolute belief, due to my own experience that night in the Catacombs. What had happened? What had caused the rift in dimensions that had allowed his presence into our world?

The spells from the old books, that's what. To be more direct, I had caused the rift, or rifts. Down there I hung the lantern from a lantern hook not too far from the entrance. I could look back and see the dim shape of the exit, and for a moment, I considered going back, and forgetting the whole thing. But it was as if I had caught some sort of infection. I was sick with curiosity, and perhaps something deeper, less identifiable that raged at my cells and crawled through my brain and tugged at that which some call a soul. I had studied too much, seen too much, and now what I knew would not let me go.

I pulled from my coat pocket a small notebook I had used to record certain spells from a variety of books, and I stood near the lantern, steeled myself to read them aloud.

What is strange, is that as I recited the spell, I misspoke a word, and for an instant, so brief it occurred in the blink of an eye, I saw a place with well-paved streets, brightly lit with powerful light. I could see machinery moving along the streets, and there were tall buildings full of glass, and people wore gay colors and those machines carried them swiftly along. I glimpsed something flying in the sky; a machine. In that earlier moment, I truly believe I saw a future that was full of light and invention. I would have done better to embrace that world, to step toward it, and possibly go there, but I was on a mission, dark and addictive.

I started the spell over, read the word correctly this time. It was all that was needed for the bright world to be sucked away and for a darker one to devour it, and leave me way down deep in the murkiest shadows of the universe. I felt cold, lonely, and empty in that moment, as if I were hanging somewhere in the dark void between the stars. It was the sort of place you would expect, down in the Catacombs, surrounded by bones, the spells of civilization gone to rot.

And then along he came, moving slowly toward me, down a corridor of stone and bones imbedded in the wall. Down the corridor he came. His narrow legs were goat-like, and its feet were stuck down through the mouths of decapitated heads splitting from supporting the great weight of the thing. He wore a top hat and had shiny needle-thin teeth and had eyes that glimmered like wet razors in moonlight—but there was no real light, just a greasy glow from the thing itself. It was a dark face, as if fashioned from coal. He wore clothes made of ragged human skins. He carried an enormous folding razor. The razor was open. He held it out in one hand and dragged it along the wall, causing sparks that jumped about like fireflies.

This was a glimpse into his world, a glimpse of him, the Lord of the Razor coming down the corridor to our world, a pathway I had opened with the spell.

The vision of the Lord of the Razor faded, all except one of the sparks, and now it floated before me, and began to move down a long tunnel, and I followed, deeper and deeper into the Catacombs.

I was looking for a box. A special box. A box hidden amidst a bone stack. There, in that box, would be what I sought. The power of the Razor. One of many made by the God, left by the God as the prize in a kind of treasure hunt for those foolish enough to pursue it.

I took hold of my lantern and continued to follow the spark, which grew brighter, but left a wake of cold air in its path.

The light in my lantern flickered. The air was not only cold, but foul, and everything around me seemed insubstantial, like a melting dream. The blue light was gone, and only the dim light of my lantern remained.

The ceiling became the floor, the floor became the ceiling. I took out the written mathematics and set them on fire with my lamp, tossed them on the ground, for that was how their power was brought into play.

I held the spell book close to the lamp, recited the Latin, and then I burnt the remains of the spells and cast them on the stone floor next to the smoldering ash of geometric symbols, the math formulas I had burned. Smoke rose blue and yellow from it. The smoke smelled of death and vinegar, perfume and sewer, sex, and destruction. Everything rocked and heaved, and then before me was a stack of skulls. The skulls at the top of the stack shook slightly, then tumbled off their perch of bone, snapped hard against the floor. Then the pile of remaining bones split open to reveal a cavern behind the bones. I placed the lantern on the ground, and went into the shadowy gap, the lantern light pulsating into the darkness, giving me dim light. I had only gone a few steps when I saw the box, not too large, white as bone, and I knew this: I had been chosen by the razor to release it. Of course, I had made this choice myself through my study, but in that moment, I felt empowered, felt the high heat of passion and greed and superiority, and it drove me onward. I felt I was the most important person in the existence of the universe, didn't realize what I should have known, that I was a patsy.

I tucked the box under my arm, started back through the bone gap and into the main cavern, nearly stumbling over the broken skulls that had rolled to the ground. I turned and looked at the breach in the bones that led to where the box had been. As I watched, the rip in space and time knitted itself up. There was only the great stack of bones before me.

All the glorious feelings of power I had felt were evaporating. In that moment, I almost cast the box from me.

Instead, I reached down for my lantern and started out of the Catacombs, the box tucked under my arm. My stomach churned, my mind reeled, the lantern light struggling to help me find a path out.

The little blue light returned. I followed it to the mouth of the Catacombs, then the light faded. I went out into the night where the air smelled and tasted cleaner and the shadows were natural and lacked weight.

My feelings of pleasure, the lifting of weight from my shoulders, lasted only until I was home. In my bedroom, sitting with one lamp lit at my desk, I decided I had made a grave mistake. I stared at the box, determined that I would never open it, that I would drop it into the river bagged up with heavy stones.

Still, I was curious.

The box was covered in designs, like scrimshaw carved into the bones. I was looking at those, realizing I had seen them in some of my books. They were the carved spells that gave power to the razor, that helped unleash it into our universe.

Then the box began to sing. The sound was sweet and sour and made the air thick and heavy. The sound rode me like a horse. I tore up, wadded up, and stuffed paper in my ears. It made no difference. I could hear the singing just as before.

I used my letter opener to pry open the box, break the lock, and inside was a great ivory-handled razor, large, but smaller than the one the God had used to make sparks in the tunnel between worlds. This was my personal razor. I reached out and touched it, received such a shock it knocked me to the ground.

The razor lay on my chest. There was a click, and it sprang open, the edge of the blade hot with light. I knew then what it wanted. Blood and souls, gathered by the cut of the razor.

I decided instantly that I must return the box. All my elation had gone away, like rain water rushing down a drain. I felt exhausted. I picked the razor carefully from my chest, folded it shut, returned it to the box and placed the box in my large desk drawer.

The drawer rattled. The razor sang.

I removed the box, placed it on the floor my closet, stacked books on top of it, and to my surprise, it ceased to sing.

I staggered to my desk chair. I remember sitting down, looking at the closed closet door, reveling in the silence.

I pulled out a journal into which I had copied containment spells. I tore the pages from the journal, carried them to the closet, tucked them into one of the books stacked onto the box.

It was my belief it would hold the razor in its place. But not forever.

I remembered a line in one of the spell books. “It eats its way free.”

***

I don’t recall going to bed, but I do know my sleep was deep, a sleep beyond the common, and in the morning, in the sunlight, everything seemed better. Feeling moderately refreshed, I went to check on my grim prize, only to find that the heavy books had collapsed on the box and caused the sides of it to break down.

With shaking hands, I removed the books, examined the box fragments. The razor was gone.

I saw a small ray of light coming through the wall, and looked. There was a rat hole there large enough for me to slide a fist through. Pushing the books aside, lying face down in the closet, I struck a match, looked through the hole in the wall. I saw the razor lying in shadow. It was open, showing its bloody blade. Bloody? How was that? It was slowly opening and closing, causing a propelling force that allowed it to crawl out of my view. It was so ridiculous I almost laughed, but that would have been like laughing at dismemberment, howling at disease.

I moved quickly.

I opened my door. Light from the windows poured into the hallway. The razor had come out of a hole in the wall, ceased crawling and lay still in the light. Tendrils of mist rose from it. Beads of blood leaked from it and spotted the floor.

I made the decision then that I should not pick it up. That I should never hold it again.

I fetched a broom and dust pan, swept it into the pan, and carried it to my room. I dropped it into a woven bag, placed it in a small empty wooden chest, along with the damaged box it had come in.

I rewrote the containment spells, as if they really mattered. I had discovered they only worked for a short time. But they were all I had.

I write this now with trepidation. I sought the razor, pursued it, and brought it away. I had felt victorious, but now I realized the victory was not mine. Victory belonged to the Lord of the Razor. I cannot let that stand. I must correct my prideful choices that have let this monstrous thing loose.

Soon, I will leave for the Catacombs, to use my spells to open the stack of bones and reveal the razor's former hiding place. I will return it. I know that's what I must do now.

Not drop it in the river. Not bury it in the ground. It must be returned to its realm.

I am growing weak from fatigue and fear, and likely from the spell of the blade. I must rest briefly, and then I must either return the blade to its source, or destroy it.

Destroy it? How?

Curiosity can be a grim mistress.

END OF JULIEN'S JOURNAL EXCERPT

While I had been reading, the rain had increased, and when I looked up from the journal, it was splattering loudly against the glass. The sky was dark and kissed with lightning. Dupin stood hands clutched behind his back, looking out at the wet world that concealed another darker world behind it.

"Disturbing," I said. "Is Julien mad, or is this real?"

Dupin turned, pursed his lips, lifted his eyes in thought.

"I think we can assume that upon completion of what he has written in his journal, he is a bit of both. Did you note the journal was dated? If not, its last entry was a few days ago. There have been two murders since then. That means he did not return the razor."

"It doesn't sound as if there is much we can do. He studied all this, he tried containment spells, and if his journal is correct, they worked poorly the first time. We have no idea if they worked the second time. You couldn't say he sounded confident."

"As schooled as he was in the occult, there is no mention in his work of what I have mentioned to you, dear friend."

"The Hounds?"

"Exactly. Though, I hasten to add, I don't know how effective they really are. Obviously, the Hounds have never truly defeated the Lord of the Razor, for he still exists. Perhaps no matter what is done to him, in one manner or the other, he will always exist. I believe, even with the Hounds, it is about containment. Consider this. The razor, he talked briefly of trying to toss it in the river or destroy it, but the thing is, the razor is as much a ghost as a solid, sharp blade."

I didn't entirely understand what Dupin meant, but I knew it couldn't be a good thing.

Dupin moved to the wardrobe, took out two white dress shirts, one mine, and one his, which meant my only dress shirt. At some point, he had painted designs on them with black paint. The designs were geometric and pictograph symbols from *The Book of Doches*, which was spread wide open on the table to serve as his artistic guide. He could have built a mouse trap at the far end of the table while I was reading Julien's journal, and I wouldn't have noticed; I had been so engrossed.

"These may provide some protection against things that come from sharp angles, or so the book says. Of course, there are no absolute guarantees, though the book speaks with confidence as to them being good temporary holding spells."

"Temporary? That's no better than Julien's spell against the razor."

"Correct. Of course, we have the paper spells, powders and the like to add to our arsenal. That said, nothing of this nature is certain, my good friend. Success is only given to those who try."

"Failure can be the companion of trying. And in this case, that one can't be undone. And he had spells as well."

"Good point," Dupin said. "I like to think I have prepared better spells while you were studying the journals. I took the liberty of reworking our weapons. The pistol ammunition, the lead balls, have been soaked in a draught made of the items I bought at the shop. I have also given them a thin coating of true silver paint, which was quite effective that time in America. The event you wrote up as the Extraordinary Case of The American Devil. I have mixed a tiny bit of the powders into our gun powder as well, though the guns will be the lesser of our weapons. Takes too long to load. I have coated the blades from our sword canes with the draught, and the silver paint. What can be done in preparation, is done."

We arrived in the rain at the Catacombs that night by cab. We carried un-lit lanterns and a large bag that Dupin called the spook bag. It was stuffed with spook items. We carried our sword canes, and our pockets were stuffed full of invocations and theorems written out in bold ink on folds of paper. Our painted shirts and pistols were covered by our coats.

Within moments of me paying the cab, we met the caretaker. He came out of a small wooden hut with one window that allowed him to see who was approaching the Catacombs. He wore a heavy coat and a wide-brimmed rain hat and a sour expression.

I felt that we should have arrived by day, but it was Dupin's point of view that doing so was pointless. The activity would be after nightfall, so that's when we should be present. I think he was driven by the challenge.

Our philosophies on such matters vary.

The caretaker, who was armed with a cane that looked designed less for walking assistance, and more for clubbing, let us into his small shack. He had a stove inside, and it was much too hot. He must have had the blood of a reptile.

Dupin paid him a small fee to let us pass after dark, when it was supposed to be closed off. There was no real hesitation on the part of the caretaker in taking the offering. We hadn't expected any, since Julien had been visiting there, obviously finding entrance after night by the same manner, the coin of the realm.

The caretaker, a watery-eyed man with a potato-sized nose, said, "I'd advise you not to. And I will soon lock the gate and leave. I don't think anything goes well in there after sunset. It is not meant to be open to the public at night, you know. I make some exceptions, of course."

"For money?" Dupin said.

"This is not a well-paying position," the caretaker said. "It's not even a position, really. There is another worker who takes up the hours when I'm gone, but I spend more time here than I prefer. I wish I liked to read. That might help. Honestly, I wish I knew how to read."

"You have had experiences here?"

The caretaker thought for a moment, said, "I personally have only heard the noises and seen the shadows. But there are stories, some I got from the previous caretaker. They were more than ghostly tales, I believe. I won't say any more than that, other to repeat that I advise against it."

"If you lock the gate," I said, "how will we get out?"

"I will give you an hour before I lock the gate, but after that, you must be out, for I will lock it, and leave."

"No concern," Dupin said. "Lock us in and leave now. I will easily get us out. I could crack a safe with my lock picking tools in less than ten minutes."

"Ten minutes is a long time if you are in need of an exit," the caretaker said.

"Your lock is not a safe. Two minutes tops for your lock."

"Still a long time, but have it your way. There was a young man that was paying me, like you. He came nightly for a time. Ceased only recently. It is no skin off my shiny ass, if you'll pardon the expression, but I tell you, he changed. Became a darker soul."

"How is that?" I asked.

"It's like you can tell a man is drunk without him staggering. You can look in his face and see it. Something worse than strong drink had settled under that young man's skin. I thought about not letting him back inside, but his money was sweet to have, as is yours."

"Did you lock him in?" I asked.

"No, but he paid more money than you, and I believe he could hardly afford it. He had what one might call a ragged gentility about him."

"Has he been here tonight?"

"No, not for a while. May God go with you, and may he have eaten a hearty dinner and have about him an extremely large gun."

The caretaker walked with us, unlocked the gate, and we slipped inside. The caretaker closed the gate behind us.

We lit our lanterns. A cold draft from nowhere and everywhere licked at the flames.

At the top and bottom of the gate there was little more than an inch of space, and the bars were narrow. The only way to exit without opening the gate or picking the lock would be to turn to smoke, an ability I wished for.

The caretaker's watery eyes seemed waterier than before. "Do you smell it?" he said.

"Of course," Dupin said.

It was an intensely sour smell carried on the cold draft.

"Lock it now," Dupin said, tapping his cane on the ground. "Right away."

The caretaker looked at him, hesitated a moment, nodded, and turned the key in the large lock. The clicking of that lock gave me an intense sensation of loneliness. It was accentuated with the sound of the caretaker's shoe heels beating away.

As we turned and started down a row of moss-coated steps, I said, "So Julien could be here?"

"If he ended up accepting the power of the razor, he could be. Or might soon be. With the Lord of the Razor's power, he could turn to mist and go through the bars of the gate, or transform himself into something that could pass through them. Rats or mice, insects."

"Obviously, Julien didn't manage to return the blade, or no longer wanted to," I said. "As you pointed out, there have been two murders since that journal entry. One on his very doorstep. The razor must have cut him, entered his soul. The blood he described on the razor, that could have been his."

"Perhaps," Dupin said.

Deeper into the Catacombs we went. The air became cooler. The odor became stronger. The lantern light hazy.

From time to time, Dupin would tuck his cane under his arm, place his lantern on the ground, and have me hold mine close to him. He pulled from his coat pocket a piece of paper, and examined it in the lantern light. Glancing over his shoulder, I saw that it was a map that he had removed, or recopied, from one of Julien's journals.

"This map only takes us so far, but I believe we have arrived at a crucial point," he said. "This is our spot. I thought it best not to open the Lord's dimensional path as early as Julien did."

Our spot was in front of a stack of skulls against a rock wall. It was different from others we had passed, and was stacked in a sort of triangle against the wall. There was about the place a feeling of crawling terror. I know how vague that sounds, but I know no other way to describe it.

Dupin folded the map, placed it in his coat pocket so carefully he made me anxious. From his other pocket, he pulled out a packet of papers, picked one, and returned the others. I could see that the paper was covered with bold drawings and there were words in a language I didn't recognize. I had faith Dupin could read it, and recite it, and probably with the proper accent.

Dupin turned to me, took a deep breath, as if he were about to dive down into deep water.

"This is the spell Julien used to open the path before, but what he didn't do was burn spell paper made by Lim Chang. I can assure you that it is far better than what Julien had. Lim Chang's paper is made from wood pulp from rotting coffins, papyrus, and the dust from mummy wrappings, sealed with glue made from blood and honey, among other concoctions.

"Destruction of the spell, if done with proper timing, raises a barrier that may be strong enough to keep the Lord of the Razor from interacting with us. I feel better schooled than Julien in this art. Does that sound pompous?"

"Of course."

"It does, does it not? Very well, we will live with that."

I didn't like the words, "may be strong enough", but I said nothing. I was curious what "proper timing" meant. The lantern I was holding vibrated. I realized my hand was shaking.

"Certainly, the burning of the spell provides temporary protection. Of that we can be certain."

"More of the temporary business," I said.

"Spells are not an exact science," Dupin said. "It's like the baker baking loaf after loaf of bread, only to find, using the same recipe, he sometimes has different results. We trust the spell recipes because we must. Our mission is to determine if the razor has been returned, or if Julien is here, soon to depart into the early night to perform his deeds for the creature."

"If he's here?"

"Then we must kill the host, bind up the parasite, and lock him back in his dimension. That will involve the Hounds, of course."

"Of course," I said. "But, do you mean tie up the Lord?"

"Not at all, you silly goose. Binding spells."

Dupin turned toward the peculiar stack of skulls. He began to chant in his deep, melodious voice. From time to time, he would lift the paper and wave it about like a lady using a handkerchief to signal a cab. Then he would stop, recite more of the spell.

I had just decided that nothing was happening, when Dupin's chanting began to feel distant. And though it was cold, I began to sweat. I experienced that which Julien had described. A sense of vertigo. Up was down and down was up, and then there was a feeling of not being exactly where we had been before. We still stood before the skulls, but all else around us seemed alien and slightly off kilter. The dark crawled. The walls were too narrow for a moment, then too wide in the next. The skull pile silently split wide. There was a large empty space in the wall behind it. No box. No razor. And, of course, no Julien.

Dupin made that peculiar clicking sound with his tongue.

"The corridor didn't open, which means the Lord is already in our world," he said. "After Julien let him out via the razor, he has stayed here in our world. Paris is a good hunting ground for blood and souls, and both of those are his singular purpose. He will return here, but I suggest we take another tack besides waiting like watch dogs.

"Still, maintain your guard. I advise you to stick close, for if you wander too far afield, the diagrams and spells on your shirt, the papers in my pocket, will not protect you. You will be unable to return to our existence. Our power is doubled when we are close together."

"I have spells in my pocket," I said.

"Yes, but I have the best ones."

"I don't know how to use the ones I have."

"Their only use is being on you. They are not burning or reciting spells. I assumed having them in your pocket you could handle. Furthermore, what aches me most is that I have miscalculated, which surprises me due to its rareness. We must hasten to Rue — to find Julien and the box, and to check on Aline."

"You think he's there?"

"I thought he would return, but he has not, so it's the next logical step. We must see if Julien is at his home, and that Aline is safe. Honestly, dear friend, it is pretty much guess work."

Dupin opened his lantern gate and stuck the paper spell against the flame. It burst into a cloud of stinking smoke and drifting ash. Dupin tossed it up, and it was consumed by fire, followed by a flurry of ashes drifting to the ground.

Instantly, the split in the skulls closed tight.

"That is most unsettling," I said.

"Indeed."

We sped away from there. The light in the lantern glowed brighter. I was relieved when I felt the sensation of walking back into our own dimensional slice. I can't say exactly when it happened, but at some point, I knew we had done just that. It felt as if we had stepped into a warmer, comfortable room.

Not being able to find a cab right away, we walked. Nightfall had well fallen by this point. The rain had ceased. It wasn't until we were well away from the Catacombs that we found a taxi. Dupin paid him extra to take us to Rue —— at as fast a pace as his horse could muster.

When we arrived at the house Julien and Aline shared, there was a lantern hung over the entrance. The street lighters had lit it much earlier, and the oil in the lamp was low. Its flame sputtered.

I hung the bag over my shoulder again, and carrying our canes and lanterns, we came to the doorway.

Dupin paused. He was staring off to one side of the porch steps.

Dupin relit his lantern, held it low. He leaned over the steps and looked at the ground. Something glimmered there. Dupin reached down and picked it up, rolled it between his thumb and finger.

"There's still dried blood on it. Oh, by all the devils and demons that we have been introduced to, my misjudging of the Catacombs is only one of my follies, for surely there is another that I have just now discovered, and it changes the situation dramatically. I should have done a thorough inspection of this area in the beginning, when we knew of the body found here."

I could see the shiny fragment clearly now. It was a wadded piece of metal. He answered my question before I could ask it.

"A fragment of cannon grapeshot," Dupin said.

I was momentarily perplexed, and then I knew. Julien had been wounded in the Battle of Valmy. Grapeshot had struck him the leg. The man who had been killed by the Lord of the Razor had died here on the doorstep, that fragment of his past torn from him, knocked into the dirt. The body that had been so horribly mauled had been Julien. And on that realization, the rest of it fell together for me.

When Julien found the razor, crawling, and singing, bloody, it had already, shall we say, bit its prey. And it was obvious now who the Lord had possessed, who its victim had been. It only took time and the nights to make the transition.

Producing the key we had obtained from Jacques, Dupin unlocked the door and started upstairs with a vigorous step.

When we reached Aline's bedroom, Dupin insisted we take off our coats to expose fully the painted designs on our shirts. I placed the bag and lantern on the floor, and removed my coat.

We took the paper spells and matches from our coats. Dupin grabbed a few items from the bag, and stuffed them into his pants pockets. We were still armed with our pistols, and we had our canes.

"We will bring one lantern," Dupin said, "and you shall carry it."

Dupin unlocked the door. I held the lantern in one hand, and with the other, lifted my cane without withdrawing the sword inside. I was prepared to strike, but I could envision the Lord of the Razor easily taking the cane from me and finding a rather uncomfortable place in which to insert it.

The outside lock worked correctly, but then we were up against the inside locks, and there was no key for that. We put our shoulders to the door, and that proved to be a bone-jarring experience. It was thick oak and well-constructed.

"Stand back," Dupin said, handing me his cane.

He backed up to the stairway, took a charging run at the door, jumped, curled his knees to his chest, and flying sideways through the air, kicked out at the door with both feet, hitting it with a sound like a clap of thunder.

Dupin, driven back by the impact, hit the floor, rolled delicately, and was instantly on his feet. He dipped a hand down and recovered a container of spell powder that had fallen from his pocket to the floor. Dupin never ceased to amaze me. It became clear to me that the long walks he took frequently had surely been spent in training in a variety of subjects other than the wearing out of shoe leather. I was the one who practiced savate, and I couldn't perform that jump and kick.

The door had broken, and fragments of it had been thrown into the room. It was wide open and dangled by one sprung hinge. Lifting the lantern into the dark, cold room, I could make out the shapes of the bed and attending furniture.

Dupin followed me inside with his lantern in one hand, and like myself, in the other he clutched his cane.

The air stank of burnt copper. There was a large stain spreading out on the floor next to the bed. It was such a large pool, we had stepped into it without noticing, and now the bottoms of our shoes were sticky with it.

Dupin made his way to the window, pulled back the curtain, let the lights of the city, the glow of the stars and moon in. He came to stand near the bed. We lifted our lanterns toward the heap on the floor.

The heap was a fragmented corpse. It was literally snapped in half like a crispy loaf of bread. The head was smashed nearly flat, and the bloody intestines were massed in a heap like a nest of snakes.

Dupin looked down to see a trail of blood running between his legs.

I saw Dupin's posture change. He bent slightly; crumple might even be the word. It was as if knots had been jerked into his spine. Quickly, he regained his posture, dropped his cane, and placed a hand in his pocket.

Slowly he turned, swinging the lantern before him.

I turned with him, and when I saw what had been lurking in the shadows behind us, what was pooled in a loop of light from the lantern, I almost collapsed. Understand, I took all of this in within seconds, but its impact was akin to suddenly finding oneself falling from a tall building when you thought you were about to take a short stair step to solid ground.

He was partially framed in shadow. He almost touched the eight-foot ceiling, the top of his crumpled black hat, anyway. He was broad of shoulder and dark as the bottom of a mine. A bloody human skin with a face was centered on the thing's chest; it was the monster's only clothing. The legs were thick at the thigh and thin at the ankle. From there its feet disappeared into the open, tooth-broken mouths of human heads. One "shoe" was a man's head, the other a woman's, her long hair wet with gore. The thing's fingernails were razors. His mouth was wide. His teeth, long, blood-wet stick pins, gleamed in the light. He held an enormous razor in one hand, and its blade dripped blood. Some of the blood ran into the symbols and shapes on the blade. In his other hand, the thing clutched a loop of blood-dripping guts. I didn't need a formal introduction to know he was the Lord of the Razor.

The designs Dupin had drawn on my shirt crawled like ants on honey.

Dupin jerked one of the geometric-covered papers from his pants pocket, flicked his lantern's gate open, and stuck the paper into the flame. The paper flared with fire.

Dupin tossed the burning paper in the Lord's direction with a flick of his wrist, called out a short spell that sounded like an oath.

As the paper floated in the air and the flame came closer to the shape, the creature hissed and dropped the loop of guts, bent as if to leap on us. Dupin tossed the lantern at the Lord. The lantern struck him hard in the chest, burst open, and the fuel and the flames ran over the monster and set him aflame. I was sure all of this was compounded by the spell that had been written on the paper.

He screamed. The flames licked at the tall hat and licked him all over. The flaming monster ran straight toward us. I was so frightened I wanted to bend over and try and crawl up my own asshole.

There was a howl from the beast that ran along my spine like a damp rat fleeing a serpent. The flaming Lord bounced back about a foot. I saw that Dupin had tossed a handful of powder in the air, and in the light given off by the burning Lord of the Razor, it was the color of sulphur. The monster stumbled back as the powder hung in the air and didn't drop. Still the monster blazed.

I remembered my spell-treated pistol. I pulled it, cocked, and fired. A space between me and the monster lit up with gunfire. Dupin followed suit. The air was soon rich with the acrid smell of gun powder and eye-watering garlic.

Our spells were working. The world slowed down. In the light created by the burning Lord of the Razor, I could see the shots of our revolvers moving forward, the air bending around them like water being parted by fish. My shot was the first, so it went through the enchanted mist and hit the Lord in the chest an instant before Dupin's missile struck.

Time jerked back into place.

Bellowing in pain, the Lord turned toward the window, rushed it, and hit it like a blazing cannon ball. The glass shattered as the Lord went through it, the flames around it gushing back toward us, and going out.

Hurrying to the window, we saw that the Lord had landed on the roof to the left of Aline's room. The fire had gone out, but smoke wisped off him and into the night, illuminated by the moonlight. The Lord rushed over the rooftop for a few yards, jumped off, and dropped still smoking to the ground.

He hit on his head-shoes, and they split, one of them breaking completely off his foot.

He left it behind, his free hoof hitting the cobblestones, the other dragging the woman's long hair behind it. He limped away into the darkness, bits of dark smoke fogging the air.

"We defeated him," I said.

"Hardly. We surprised him. Next time he won't be so unaware, unsuspecting of our preparations. We still have one serious card to play, however. The Hounds."

I rushed to the doorway and grabbed the lamp that we had left behind, turned and lifted it with a shaky hand. I inched forward, held it over the blood-soaked ruin on the floor.

"Poor Aline," I said.

"That's not Aline," Dupin said, taking my lantern from me, holding it over the corpse. "It's Jacques. I recognize a piece of his face. Look there at the edge of the bed."

I looked. A patch of face with nose and whiskered cheeks. Yes. Jacques.

"Jacques came back for his money, certainly before nightfall, but here in the dark room, the

Lord was still powerful. He opened the door and let Jacques in, and it wasn't money that Jacques collected, it was murder."

"Can Jacques now turn into a razor-wielding creature?"

"There can only be one at a time in any dimension, and the one that exists now just exited the room. It was she who was cut, and it was she the razor sought out. That's why Julien was killed on the doorstep. He was trying to leave with it. But the razor had already claimed its host. It was Aline who was cut when the razor escaped Julien's box, and it is her that we must now pursue."

"Surely that can't be her."

Dupin went to the closet and opened it. Swung the lantern inside, kicked a hat box on the floor aside.

There was a mouse hole in the wall.

"When it escaped the box, it entered here, and somehow, perhaps exploring a noise in the closet, Aline was cut. Remember her limp when she came to see us."

"But she was okay."

"It wasn't night. She was unaware of what had happened. But when night came, all she had to do was open the window and exit as she just now did. At the Catacombs she killed her first victim. Perhaps there are others we know nothing about."

"But how did the razor end up in the hall, where Julien grabbed it?"

"I can't say for sure. I wouldn't be surprised if she kicked at it when it cut her, and it went back through the hole and slid out into the hall. The hole in Julien's room had allowed its initial escape, and the hole in Aline's closet allowed her to be cut. My guess is she thought she had stepped on something. And she had. The Lord's razor. It seemed inconsequential to her at the time, but she was infected. And in time, it would come to her and sing and offer itself to her, and she was persuaded. Julien, perhaps due to his spells, avoided being cut, but if Aline had not been, it was just a matter of time until he was. They had both been doomed the moment Julien read those old, horrid books of magic and spells."

The realization hit me as hard as if a building had fallen on me. I couldn't imagine that the beautiful Aline had been overtaken by such a horrid spirit. That she had cut her own brother and Jacques up the way she had. It was brain numbing.

"To help her," Dupin said, "we must destroy what she has become. We must hurry."

Dupin's voice was kind and soft, a rare tone for him. I nodded.

We paused to slip on our coats, reload our pistols, and grab the spook bag, and then went away from the house and hustled along the route the monster had gone. The air stank of fire and brimstone, blood, and decay. It was a trail we could follow as surely as an American frontiersman might follow the sign of a beaver or a bear.

Along the Seine we went, the river a ribbon of silver in the moonlight. We broke away from that path and followed the fading stench. Not that we needed to. Dupin knew where the Lord was going.

The Catacombs.

The Catacomb gate was locked, but from the smell of toasted Lord in the air, it was evident that it had entered the Catacombs.

Dupin had to pick the lock. When he pushed aside the gate, the squeaking of the hinges seemed frighteningly loud, and if ever the Lord might need an alarm that we had arrived, that would serve.

Dupin broke out the map. I held the lantern while he examined it.

"We have been to our destination before, but I believe the map is more certain," he said. "I think the path to the Lord of the Razor might be more twisty than expected; that it changes from visit to visit, if one is so foolishly inclined. That includes us, obviously."

"Obviously."

"In fact…"

Dupin held the map out to me. I looked. It was different than earlier. The lines on it had been resituated.

"The map has a spell on it, old friend."

It was almost more than I could accept. After a short study of the map, we went down the interior steps, into the bone-lined darkness.

As we proceeded, Dupin pulled out some of the spell papers and lit them from my lantern. When he tossed them, the dust motes in the air caught fire and blushed with blue-white blazes that flickered and sputtered and moved. We followed them as they gusted along a path lined with skulls and bones.

"Spectral homing pigeons," Dupin said.

As before the air became colder and fouler. The walls of the cavern closed in on us, so close that my coat sleeve brushed the skulls and bones as we passed. This was followed by the former disorientation I had experienced, and that Julien had mentioned in his journal. Up was down and down was up. I swear for a short time, we were walking sideways on the wall, our feet resting on the skulls as we went.

And then we were in a cavern and the wall before us came open. It was replaced with a long, rocky corridor. There was a scraping sound, a breathing sound like someone sucking air through a tube. Then there were bright sparks, bright enough to light up the dimensional corridor, as well as the one in which we stood. A whiff of toasted Lord of the Razor was strong in the air.

"Here we make our fight," Dupin said.

I slung the spook bag off my shoulder, placed it on the ground. I knew what was coming. I pulled my pistol. It had worked before, along with spells and a tossed lantern. But on our way to the Catacombs, Dupin assured me that the Lord would have learned from experience, and this time out, he would be ready.

He opened the spook bag and took out a thick piece of chalk treated with spells and powders and phosphorescence. As he drew a circle around us, the chalk glowed in the dark.

There was a sound in the corridor. A scratching sound. Then squeaking.

What came down the corridor was not the Lord of the Razor. At least not in his common form. What came were large, squeaking, chattering rats the size of dogs. They came fast, and when they leaped out of the tunnel and in our direction, they glowed blue. When they hit the outside of our circle, they burst into flames, puffs of hair blowing into non-existence, yellow rat teeth clattering to the cavern floor outside the circle.

"Squeak that," Dupin said.

In the tunnel the rats, their number having grown to epic proportions, became a squealing wall of rats, floor to ceiling. Their yellow-stained teeth were highlighted by our lantern's glow and the popping blue sparks that drifted about like malignant pixies.

Their appearance shifted and they were now the Lord of the Razor, wearing an outfit of rat skins, a rat skin top hat tilted on his head. He had one foot in the female head, and the other had been replaced by a skull from the Catacombs. The Lord smiled its stick-pin teeth at us.

"Oh, the fun I will have with you," the Lord of the Razor said in Aline's voice, and hearing her voice coming out of such a monster sickened me.

"Stay strong and alert. The Lord is a trickster," Dupin said. "But so am I."

The pile of bones shifted. Skulls rolled to the dirt floor, snapping their teeth. Leg bones and arm bones rattled against the dirt so severely there were numerous clouds of dust.

The rat-constructed Lord of the Razor moved one foot forward, wiggled his head-shoe foot against the chalk line. There was a roar of knee-high flame from all around the circle. The Lord was not bothered. The woman's much abused head caught fire. Flames erupted from its now empty eye-sockets, gushed out of its open mouth, turning the woman's ruined teeth to smoking nubs. Popping blazes ran all around our chalk circle.

The Lord of the Razor shook his foot until the flames on the smoldering head puffed to smoke. The fire around the circle went dead and the chalk line was no longer white. It was black and littered with ash.

Dupin poured dark powder from one of the vials. The powder spread wider than seemed possible for the contents of that vial. It puffed all around our feet.

He said a quick spell in some language so foreign it might have been what green cheese men speak on the moon. He ended his invocation with, "Bite his ass off."

The powder swirled, formed six mounds of dirt on the ground, as if moles were pushing it up from below. The space was so taken up by them, we were backed up to the rear of the charred circle.

There was a coughing sound from the mounds. Dust filled the circle from floor to ceiling. I had to close my eyes and cover my mouth and nose with my hand to keep from being overwhelmed by it.

The dust cleared, and where there had been mounds, now there were azure-colored creatures. They were long and lean and appeared to be wearing armor. A closer look revealed it to be crustaceous scales. They had long pink proboscis that wiggled. They had whiskers like wire, and their faces appeared to be crusted with mange. They had slits for eyes. They barked like dogs. The Hounds of Tindalos.

They leaped from the circle, passing through it, making the air around the circle waver like a mirage.

The Lord's odd eyes showed something I didn't expect. Fear? Surprise?

The Hounds hit the rat-made Lord with their leap, their flashing dagger-shaped teeth snapping. Gouts of oily, dark blood gushed from the monster, hit the invisible wall of the circle. And wall it was. Solid from bottom to top. The barrier dripped with greasy gore. It was as if we were watching it through a window glass, instead of seeing it trickle against an invisible barrier.

"There are twelve Hounds," Dupin said, grinning at me.

Pulling another vial from the bag, he shook it, poured darkness from it, repeated the previous spell. The dirt in the circle mounded again. The dust rose. The dust parted. Six new Hounds leaped effortlessly through the invisible wall, disrupting the beads of dripping blood that coated it. Now all twelve Hounds were snapping and biting at the Lord. His dark blood was running in torrents on the stone floor, splashing on the piles of bones. It flowed then pooled around our circle and quickly crusted like a scab.

The rats that made up the Lord broke apart, and of course, so did the Lord. The rats ran in all directions. Over the piles of bones. Under the bones. Through cracks in the wall. Even with their absence, I could feel the presence of the Lord of the Razor, the way you can feel and taste an incoming electrical storm.

"Now, let's hope this works," Dupin said, and pulled his sword, tapped the ground at the edge of the circle, recited a brief spell.

I was reminded the sword had been coated in a powder, and powered with spells.

"Draw your own, do as I do."

I did just that, tossing the exterior shell of the cane aside. I tapped the tip of my sword on the dirt and stones in the circle.

"No," Dupin said. "Tap the edge of the circle."

I did that while Dupin repeated the spell. My sword vibrated in my hand. I could feel power running through it. The chalk circle turned white again and a thin blue light surrounded the circle, enveloping us in its spell.

"If this works, it will protect us from the Hounds. If they become bored with the Lord, or distracted from him, they will turn on us. He is their natural enemy, but after him, everything, and everyone else, is their foe."

In that short time the Lord had reformed into his original horrible glory, no rats. A ghostly version of Aline floated out of him and dissolved with a fizzling sound, became flat and drifted to the ground like a fallen leaf. Then the thin shell of her melted into the earth and was gone. We had not destroyed the Lord, but the Hounds and Dupin's spells had caused it to discard her sheath. He was through with her.

The God was gleefully swinging its razor, chopping the Hounds into meat and broken scales. But the meat slithered wetly over the floor, rejoined with other fragments, and fused. The scales crackled and moved. Within instants, the Hounds were back together, their proboscis wiggling in the air.

The battle went on. The Hounds drove the Lord back to the opening in the dimensional gap, and with one last swing of his razor, a swing that cut a Hound half in two, it stepped back into its dimensional pathway. Instantly, piles of bones slammed together. There was a sound like faraway thunder. The slamming of the pathway cut one of the Hounds in two, shooting sticky mess out of its rear end, causing its ribs to snap through its flesh and armor.

The rest of the Hounds were barred from following. They snapped and shattered skulls and bones in their anger. They began to howl. That howl resembled that of a wolf, but it went so much deeper into the flesh and bones. The howls seemed to be spiked with needles.

"Now, my friend, things might become testy," Dupin said.

As he spoke, he was tossing another vial of powder into the air. The powder, once tossed, hung in place like a gray gauzy curtain, surrounding us within the circle.

The Hounds came at us, leaped against the circle and were bounced back. And then they began to chew close to the ground. The circle was coming loose; they were snapping its contents down their throats. There was only the hanging powder inside the circle to protect us. I thought I could see a change on their faces, a kind of smug satisfaction. They had us now.

Or so they thought. They lunged against the hanging powder, and were bounced back.

"It will not hold for long," Dupin said. "It is another temporary barrier."

"Don't you have anything more permanent?"

"Perhaps." He bent and pawed about in the open spook bag. He came out with a small box, said, "Explosives. Along with a spell."

Before I could ask if this was really the proper choice, he opened the top of the box, revealing a fuse. He pulled a match, said, "You might want to cover your ears and tighten your ass sphincter." He scratched the match alight, lit the fuse, and tossed the box. It went through the grimy barrier effortlessly and exploded.

The explosion blew away from us in a wall of green flame and washed over the Hounds, filling everything in sight. The triangle of skulls and bones charred and puffed to the ground. The Hounds were knocked back, thrown about like ripped rag dolls. And then they were gone.

"You killed them," I said.

"No. I sent them home. I wasn't sure that would work, but it did. Like the Lord of the Razor, they still exist in their dimension, but perhaps they are barred for a time, before some idiot allows them back into our world."

The barrier of powder fell to the floor with a sound like dropped gravel.

"And just in time," Dupin said.

"And what of Aline?" I asked.

"My dear friend, there is no more Aline. But her essence has been successfully pulled from him. Her soul, if you prefer. It is free, and she is no longer his slave in any manner, shape or form. It's not perfect, but it is better than the dark alternative. Where the Lord lives, the souls he's taken to deposit there are not in a good place. Everything evil flows through them like soured milk, their bodies are full of blisters and wounds, scabs for mouths, noses, and eyes. Their nerves and flesh and bones are like constantly vibrating cables filled with pain. We have allowed Aline to avoid that. It is as good an outcome as can be expected."

That night we dined on cold meat and cheese and cups of black coffee. We sat in our living quarters, quiet for long stretches, with only the sounds of our cups and saucers scraping and rattling.

"So, will the Lord be back?"

"As I said, if some idiot summons him, he will, and believe me, this universe is full of curious idiots. He promises power. And he has it, and perhaps you might gain some of it, but in the end that power has teeth and it bites the very person who opened the gate to our world."

"I can't get over Aline being taken away like that."

"You wanted it to all end like a fairy tale, did you not?"

"I suppose I did."

"Life isn't like that, dear friend. It goes its own path without our consultation. Accept this, old friend. We were able to stop its presence in our world and do good for Aline. And remember, sad as it is, Julien is to blame for her loss, and his own. He realized that too late, and there was nothing he could do about it."

"But you could, and did."

"This time. I have a certain amount of informative experience. I have been around the sun more times than you might suspect," Dupin said. "But that is for another discussion. There was one other thing I had to assist me in this horrid endeavor besides a lifetime of experience, and it was the essential component in sending the Lord back to his kingdom."

"The Hounds?"

"They helped. But they were not the true key."

"Then what?"

"Why, my dear friend. I had a powerful secret weapon."

"Secret weapon?"

He smiled at me.

"I had you."